W9-AYH-124

DISCARD

Who wants a cheap Rhinoceros?

Revised and expanded edition

By Shel Silverstein

Macmillan Publishing Co., Inc., New York
Collier Macmillan Publishers, London

*Revised and expanded edition of a work
previously published under the pseudonym "Uncle Shelby"*

Macmillan Publishing Co., Inc.
866 Third Avenue, New York, N.Y. 10022
Collier Macmillan Canada, Inc.
Printed in the United States of America

10   9   8   7   6   5   4   3   2   1

Library of Congress Cataloging in Publication Data
Silverstein, Shel.
   Who wants a cheap rhinoceros?
   Summary: There are lots of things a rhinoceros
can do around one's house, including eating bad
report cards before one's parents see them,
tiptoeing downstairs for a midnight snack,
and collecting extra allowance.
   [1. Rhinoceros—Fiction]   I. Title.
PZ7.S588Wh 1983   [E]   82-23945
ISBN 0-02-782690-2

To Meg and Curt

Who wants a cheap rhinoceros?
I know of one for sale,
With floppy ears and cloppy feet,
And friendly waggy tail.
He's sweet and fat and huggable.
He's quiet as a mouse.
And there are lots of things that he
Can do around your house.

For instance...

You can use him for a coat hanger.

He is a terrific back scratcher.

And he makes a very lovely lamp.

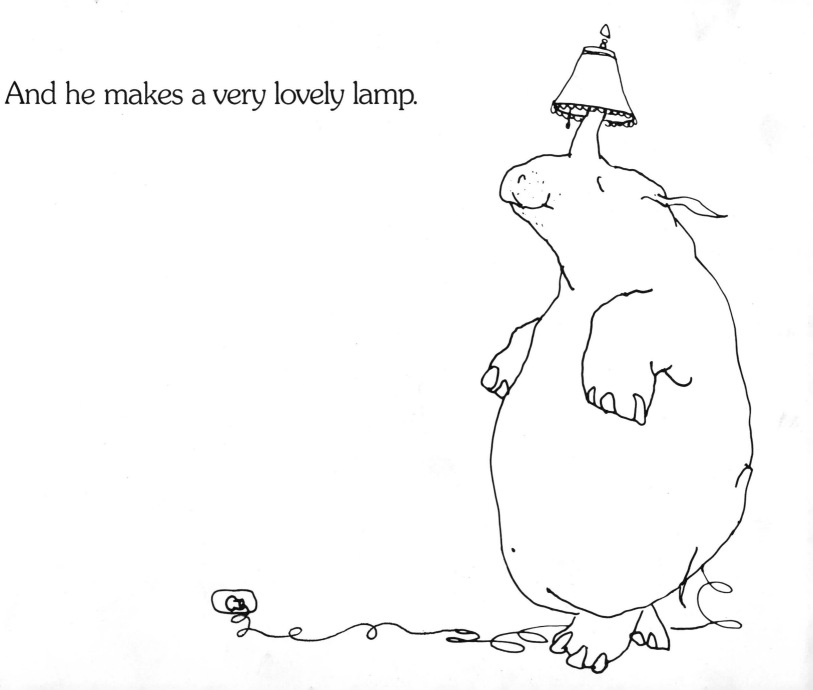

He will eat bad report cards before your parents see them.

But he is not too great at opening doors.

He makes a good bloody ferocious pirate.

He can open beer cans for your uncle.

And on Sunday
you can read him
the comics.

He will be glad to turn a jump rope...

...if he gets his turn.

He's not too careful about watching where he walks.

But he's very handy for collecting extra allowance from your father.

He makes an unsinkable battleship.

But he is not too interested in taking his bath.

It is
very
comfortable
when
you sit
on his
lap,

but
not too
comfortable
when
he sits
on your
lap.

He's terrific at helping
your grandmother make donuts.

118872

And he is great for not letting your mother hit you when you haven't really done anything bad.

He is very nice about crawling into bed
with you on cold winter nights,

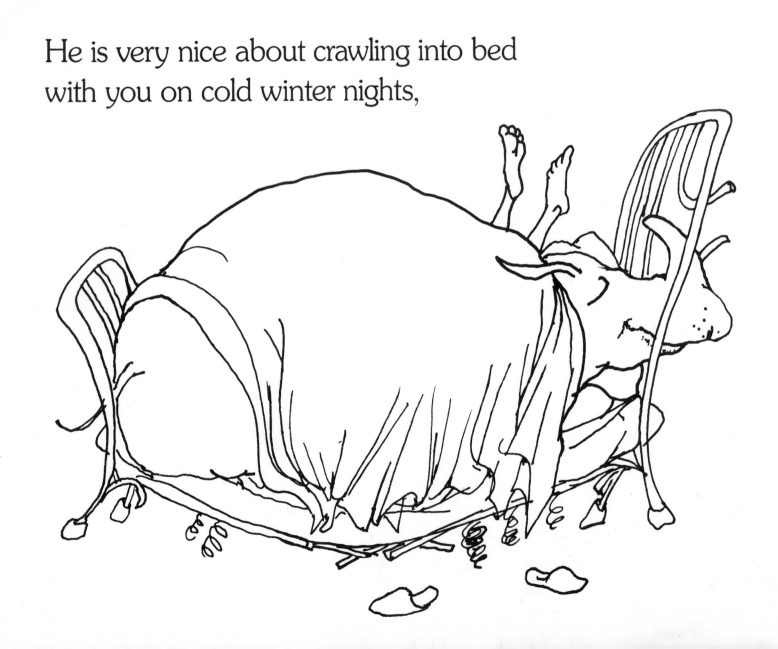

and he is pretty good at
tiptoeing downstairs
for a midnight
snack.

And he'll gladly eat scraps from the table.

He is terrific at being Ben and Charlie,
two desperate crooks.

And he loves to surprise you.

He will be glad to help your aunt
knit a sweater.

Especially if it is for him.

He is careful about not leaving rhinoceros
tracks around the house.

He is fun to take care of
when he is sick.

And he is great for
plowing your field
if you are a
farmer.

He is hard
to build a
house for.

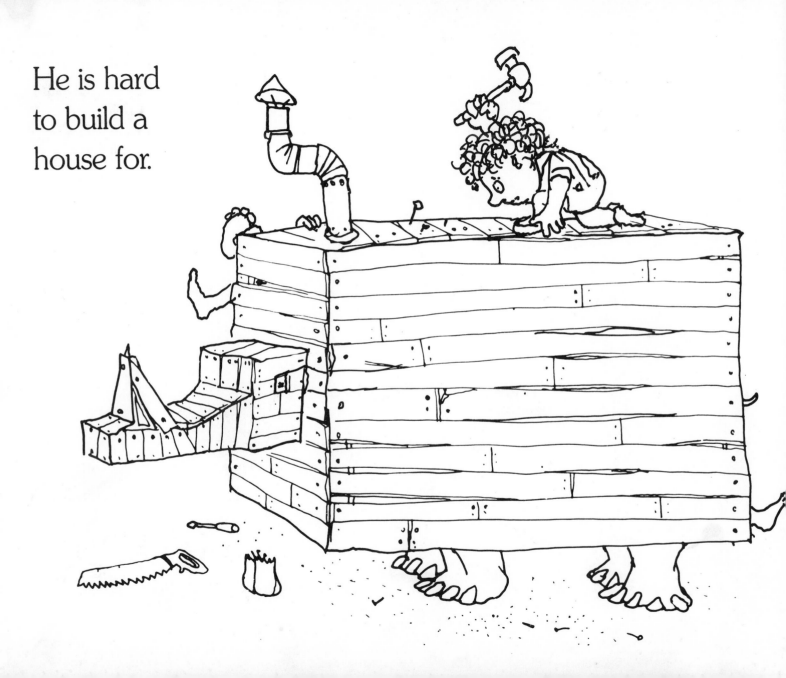

But he is lots of fun
at the beach

because he is great at imitating a shark.

He is wonderful
for playing records
if you have
no phonograph.

And on Halloween you can dress him up
like a girl—but he won't like it.

He loves to play
hide and seek.

He is good for yelling at.

And he is easy to love.